Personal Letters

- Before Beginning to write a Letters
- Invitation Letters
- Letters of Sympathy
- Congratulation Letters
- Letters of Recommendation
- Disrepute Letters

Written by
Arun Sagar 'Anand'

Translated by
Editorial Board

V&S PUBLISHERS

Published by:

V&S PUBLISHERS

F-2/16, Ansari road, Daryaganj, New Delhi-110002
☎ 23240026, 23240027 • *Fax:* 011-23240028
Email: info@vspublishers.com • *Website:* www.vspublishers.com

Regional Office : Hyderabad
5-1-707/1, Brij Bhawan (Beside Central Bank of India Lane)
Bank Street, Koti, Hyderabad - 500 095
☎ 040-24737290
E-mail: vspublishershyd@gmail.com

Branch Office : Mumbai
Jaywant Industrial Estate, 2nd Floor–222, Tardeo Road
Opposite Sobo Central Mall, Mumbai – 400 034
☎ 022-23510736
E-mail: vspublishersmum@gmail.com

Follow us on:

All books available at **www.vspublishers.com**

Publisher's Note

It gives us pleasure to publish this book on letter writing named **Personal Letter**. It had been our cherished desire to bring out a book on letter writing for readers in a systematic and scientific manner.

This book attempts to present rules for letter writing in all possible situations and circumstances. Despite the availability of e-mails, telephones, mobile phones, instant messaging, etc., it is ultimately the correspondence made through letters that matters. Letters have retained their preponderance in a milieu of communications the way books have remained strong among all readable materials – whether available in printed or digital forms.

Using words in simple and day-to-day language, this book tries to exemplify every kind of letters ordinarily people take recourse to while writing on personal subjects.

We sincerely hope the readers would make the best use of this book to master the art and science of letter writing in all situations and circumstances.

Contents

Letter Writing

L etter writing has become an important component in social life. The world appears to be interconnected by one way or another. No one has the time to meet another person as much as one would wish.

Letter writing is as old as humanity. Pigeons were used to carry messages in early times. There existed no postal facility then. Things moved on but what didn"t change course was the means of letter writing.

A person can continue to be in touch with another person, wherever he may be, by means of letters. Psychological studies reveal that:

❑ A person wants to preserve whatever he things or visualizes. He wants to share this with someone close. This he can do by means of communicating through letter writing.

❑ People who have spent years in jail reveal that but for maintaining touch with friends and relatives by letter writing, their thought processes, which is alive and kicking, would have dried up long ago.

❑ Pandit Jawaharlal Nehru"s letters to his daughter Indira Gandhi has become historical in true sense. Its relevance is for the posterity. That"s one reason why letters of great people are compiled for the benefit of the coming generations. Letters written by Lenin, Churchill, Mussolini, Napoleon, Hitler and Abraham Lincoln have made them immortal.

❑ Letter writing protects one from excitement, emotions, anger, etc. It is said that Abraham Lincoln used to start writing letters whenever angry. He would download his anger using the means of letter writing. Such letters he would always, instead of sending to the intended recipient, read and reread later to analyse what made him angry in the first place.

❑ If a person talks about his pain, ordinarily others wouldn"t pay much attention. Instead, they would act out the 'sympathy" part. No real feelings. But when the same pain is put down in writing, others try to understand the underlying idea behind the anguish and work out ways to help out.

❑ Letters strengthen the bonds among people. Pen-friendship is a testimony to this fact. People across the world can learn about one another. This helps strengthen cultural and social ties.

Letter writing is a reflection of times. A letter written today may have words like mobile phone, computer, television, google, facebook, internet, etc. We can, similarly, know about the history or geography of one country or another. Dress habits, culture, etc. get mirrored through letters.

Mentioned below are a few points we must take into consideration while writing:

❑ Nothing should be written that may compromise the social harmony.

❑ Letters must keep one another"s interest in mind.

❑ Letters should focus primarily on human welfare and not politics.

❑ Nothing irrelevant should find space in a letter.

❑ The language used should be easy and simple.

❑ A letter should reflect honesty; not hypocrisy.

❑ A letter should be brief and to the point.

Letter Writing: An Art

L etter writing has a bearing on our personal and social life. They reflect the way we conduct ourselves in society. To know a person, reading a few letters written by him is enough. Letters would reveal the working and thought process of his mind at different times in different situations. The letters symbolise the psychology, emotions, sense of belongings, personal relations and social equations, a person maintains.

A person has become a combination of various pulls and pressures. This finds expression though correspondence. Without letters or other modes of communications, it is difficult to maintain equilibrium in friendship, relations, social mores, work culture, business, polity, etc. The success and failure in life also depends a great deal upon our methods of correspondence. The more successful one is in letter writing, the more successful he is likely to become in future.

The habit of letter writing starts developing right from the student life. Such letters are written to parents, teachers and friends. These reflect the bonds of emotional attachment.

As soon as one enters the adult life, the letters acquire the edge of love, feelings and attachment.

Where personal relations are concerned, letters mostly portray closeness and empathy.

If you want to become a prolific letter writer, please pay attention to the following:

❑ Letter should be logical, short, crisp and clear.

❑ The presentation should be scientific, not full of emotions. Official and managerial letters should be built around solid matters, straightforward and to the point.

❑ The letter should be developed around proper reference and context. It must be clear, else confusion may arise. Before dispatching a letter, one should read it as if the receiver is reading it. Check everything is clear and accurate. If not, make changes where necessary.

❑ Never write a letter when angry.

❑ Always take care of your goodwill.

❑ A letter should be balanced, short and precise.

3

Before Beginning to Write a Letter

A letter is an image of the writer, his attitude, his personality. A letter is talk upon paper; but it is not as easy to write as it is to tell your story in spoken words, because when you talk, your audience is before you, and you can better adapt your words to the receiver who is present, than to one who is absent. If what you say when you talk is not right, and does not have the desired effect, you are likely to have opportunity to explain. What you say in a letter, however, must stand as it is, and is not subject to immediate correction, change or even a 'retake" much like we have in films. Therefore, the letter must be prepared with more care, and with more attention to detail, than is necessary for the spoken word.

It has been said, and with much truth, that nobody can write a letter, or any document, which is guaranteed to be fully and correctly understood by its receiver. The letter writer, therefore, must do his best, for the more care he gives to his letter, the greater likelihood there is of its being properly interpreted by its receiver.

Perfection is impossible, but there is a vast difference between a carelessly thrown-together letter and one which is intelligently written. A large part of the business of the world is conducted by correspondence; and no one can maintain his position without the writing of social letters.

While this book attempts to present rules for letter writing, it must be admitted that outside of the fundamental principles, it is difficult to instruct any one so that he may become, by these instructions alone, a prolific letter writer. Individual judgement and common sense play important parts upon the stage of letter writing. One may be helped by suggestions, and even by rules; but instruction alone is not sufficient. He must put himself into his letters. Proficiency exists only when one realizes their importance, and lets each experience aid him in producing better results. The book doesn"t aim to present more than a few forms of the body of a letter, because such arbitrary examples would be of little use to any proficient letter writer; and the indifferent one, using them, would make his letters framed and confined. One should, then, become familiar with suitable forms, and should adapt them to his conditions, but should not copy verbatim the style or wording of this book or any other for that matter.

A letter writer must keep the following in mind:

Clarity

A letter writer should be clear about the subject matter of the letter. It should be in plain and simple language so that the reader immediately gets to the bottom of the content. Confusion should be avoided at all costs.

Fullness/Absoluteness

Not only a letter should be clear in explaining things, but it should be complete as well. Nothing should be written that is out of context, nor any topic should be repeated. If something comes to mind after the letter has been written, then P.S.(Post Script) written below the letter serves the purpose. The subject missed out of the main letter is mentioned in P.S.

Ease

Simplicity is the lifeblood of any letter. It must be written with ease and appear logical moving from one idea to another. Difficult words have to be avoided. Small and short sentences make a letter easy to understand.

In Short

Brevity is the soul of a letter. It should also be complete in all respects without missing out on anything relevant. Unnecessary verbosity mars the ease in understanding the text matter.

Effective

Words must be used with care and caution. Only popular words and in current usage convey the meaning to an average reader. Letter should be interesting so that the recipient finds it interesting to read.

Manners

Language used should be polite and full of respect and etiquette. Courtesy breeds courtesy. Correct salutations make for a prompt reply. This fact must not be overlooked under any circumstances.

Attractive

Appearance of a letter enhances its attraction, makes it more readable, and sub-consciously forces the reader to take note of the contents. The language of the letter deserves careful attention. Name and address should be written with accurately. No one likes to see his name misspelt.

Paper

A good quality paper draws the attention of the reader and makes for a good impression. Whereas students tend to use colourful and fancy papers, the grown-ups go for good quality plain papers. Ordinary papers are good enough for day-to-day mails; light-weight papers should be preferred for air mails. This reduces the expenses on postage.

Pen & Ink

Coloured inks, other than blue or black, should be used only during special occasions. Coloured inks don"t find approval from most people.

Writing with a pencil is a big No, while writing a letter. They become difficult to read or make out. *Therefore, every letter should be written with a pen.*

Accuracy & Cleanliness

Every sentence must be complete and carry a definite meaning. It should be easy to read and understand. While writing a business letter, special care must be taken regarding a bill, *hundi,* book of accounts, other commercial details, failing which the goodwill of the firm may be compromised.

Satisfactory

The credibility of a business letter hinges on the clarity and completeness with regard to details. Confusion at all costs should be avoided. The letter must clearly mention the weight, price, type, quality, amount and discount regarding the product. Making a mention of the available guarantee increases the value of the product and enhances the image of the firm.

Systematic

Points raised in the letter should follow an established sequence. Only one issue should be mentioned under a single point. Long sentences must be avoided. The letter, if necessary, should be made attractive by going in for an additional paragraph.

At Proper Time

Delay hurts a business and its growth. It hits the image of the firm as well. Letters should be promptly replied. If it is not possible to reply with sought-after information, an acknowledgement of the letter must be sent. Make a point to apologise, if for any reason, reply couldn"t be made in time.

Planning

A letter should be properly planned before writing. *Clarity is of utmost importance.* The reader must comprehend the subject matter of the letter. Respectful and polite words make the reader favourably inclined towards the writer.

Writing

A letter reflects the personality of the writer. Hence, it is important for a writer to be careful in the choice of words or sentences.

A letter may give out the establishment and line of organization, a writer has in his work ethics. *Good style and polished manners leave a sound impression on the recipient.*

Envelope

An envelope should be carefully chosen, capable of reflecting the image of the sender. The name of the recipient should begin close to the centre of the envelope and about one inch below the top edge. It should be followed by C/O (where required). This should be followed by House No, Lane, Locality, Name of the town/city, PIN Code, etc.

We can write Mr/Mrs/Sri/Smt, etc. before the name of a gentleman/lady. 'Esq" is often written before the name of any distinguished person. For an unmarried girl, the term, 'Miss" is used. Whereas 'To" is written in English, the term, 'Sewa Men" is used in Hindi.

Beginning to Write a Letter

While writing a letter, the writer should mention his 'address" on the top right hand side of the paper. This is followed by the 'date" right below the address. If the address is already printed on the paper, there is no need to write the address afresh. The name and address of the recipient is written on the left side of the paper. The form of writing is mainly used in business correspondence. It facilitates the office clerk to enter the sender"s and recipient"s address in the dispatch register. However, in personal letters, the address of the recipient is not written.

Subject of the Letter

There is little point elaborating at this stage on the subject matter of a letter. This is fully explained in subsequent chapters. It is enough to understand that it is the 'subject" that necessitates writing of any letter. The subject is the reason for entering into any correspondence. We have compiled a series of letters in the following pages taking note of various circumstances that directly or indirectly suggest us to write a letter. The readers would be able to understand the manner and presentation of writing letters in the most appropriate and modern style.

Correct Style of Writing

The writer must choose words with care. A word wrongly used could change the meaning of the letter altogether. The meaning of the letter may become confusing or even irrelevant. The words that convey the intended meaning should only be used.

Similarly, the writer should pay attention to the *accuracy of the words also.* Correct spellings of the words are important. Unlike spoken words, there is no chance to recall the word that has been put down. The letter will stay as it is, wrong words, unintended words or confusing words. You can"t wish them away. Therefore, be careful while using any word.

Use of Comma

Sometimes placing a 'comma" at a wrong place can change the meaning of the sentence. You wanted to convey one thing but by placing the 'comma" at a wrong place, the idea gets changed. In fact, even the opposite meaning could also be conjured up. The writer must put a full stop after completion of a sentence. An explanatory sign is marked as ('!"). While quoting someone else"s sentence, inverted comma ('...") is indicated. Mark of interrogation ('?") is used whenever the sentence asks for an answer.

Typing Letters

Some opine that personal letters shouldn"t be typed. Intimacy is lost and formality is introduced. But many people have started sending personal letters duly typed. The advantage typed letters introduce is ease in reading and simplicity in capturing the theme.

Business Letters

The major difference between success and failure of a business is attributed to the way correspondence is done. *Writing business letters is a great art.* It is considered important to make correspondence in a timely manner; and without delay. Business letters are divided into following five sections:

1. Sales-related correspondence
2. Day-to-day regular correspondence
3. Accounts-related correspondence
4. Advertisement-related correspondence
5. Establishment-related correspondence

The above mentioned letters can be sub-divided into many other sections. Irrespective of sections or sub-sections, every correspondence ultimately ends up contributing to sales. No letter should be delayed in responding quickly, more so a business one. *A prompt reply boosts a firm"s image.* Moreover, it is a matter of courtesy and business ethics.

Business letters should preferably be typed. Many large organisations make use of a shorthand writer to dictate letters for eventual typing.

Closing a Letter

Whereas in English language, letters written in the first person close with the words, 'Yours Truly" or 'Yours faithfully", the corresponding Hindi words are 'Aapka" or 'Tumhara". 'Aapka" is used only as a mark of respect for an elder person. Form of closing a letter requires more care and attention in business letters than in personal ones.

Business Signature

Business letters should be signed such that the recipient finds practically no difficulty in deciphering his name. If the writing is illegible, his name should be clearly typed below the signature.

Goodwill of the Firm

An attractive manner of letter writing impresses the recipient and enhances the goodwill of the firm. Care must be taken to see that the image of the firm gets a leg-up with every correspondence.

Letter Writing and its Importance

L etter writing is a process of exchanging communications by means of letters. It could be between two firms, organisations, customers, or personal relations. It could be between a firm and a customer. In fact, any exchange of ideas between two individuals or entities is broadly classified as *correspondence through letters.*

Importance of Letter Writing

Letters are an important form of communication. It is a medium to exchange views. Following points constitute the major components of letter writing:

❑ **Written medium of expression** – Letter is a medium of exchange of ideas between two letter writers. It can be resorted to when inconvenience is experienced while making any oral communication.

❑ **Simplicity in record keeping** – It is difficult to keep a record of oral discussions. But a written communication can be conveniently filed for future reference. It can be gone through as and when required.

❑ **Opportune time to use considered thoughts** – It sometimes happens that we speak something that we never intended to say. But a letter writer saves himself from such undesirable situations. If a word has been erroneously written, it can always be amended, modified and reset for improved impression.

❑ **Continuity in relationship** – Letters help in cementing the relationship between two persons or firms even if they are not meeting each other on a regular basis.

❑ **As a representative** – *A letter in essence is a representative of the writer.* While a personal letter represents an individual, a business letter does the same for an organisation.

❑ **As a medium of complaint** – *A complaint made orally is not as effective as a written one.* A written one stands testimony to the proof that some difficulty or inconvenience is experienced against which redressal has been sought. It forms part of a complaint register.

❑ **Conveyor of pleasure and pain** – A letter is a communication that can convey good news or an inconvenient one. It acts as a postman who can bring in news of all sorts – good, bad or ugly.

❑ **Government"s messages** – The government circulates its orders, information, news, etc. through the medium of letters.

- ❑ **Proof** – The letters stand proof of a document circulated or conveyed.

- ❑ **As a literature** – Writers write books, notes, novels, poems, etc. and place before the general public for recreation, or information or enjoyment. This eliminates the sense of loneliness.

- ❑ **As a social reformer** – Various newspapers and magazines earmark space for people to write their views, comments or complaints against the ills existing in the society. The columns represent both, the bouquets and the brickbats.

- ❑ **As a critic** – Letters are means of critical appreciation written by a reader of any literary work or happening of common public importance.

- ❑ **Economic medium** – In these days of busy life, letters are a very economical medium to remain in touch with family, friends and relatives. They are equally useful in maintaining business relationships.

5

Invitation Letters

There are many occasions when a person wishes to invite others to celebrate some memorable moments. Inauguration, marriage, *griha pravesh*, birthday, etc., are some of those occasions.

If the occasion demands compassion or condolence, a letter to such effect can convey the feeling adequately. Sometimes, we commit some blunder, though unintentionally, and come to realise later. In such situations, it is quite appropriate to seek forgiveness. At times, we can"t make it to the place, despite our wanting to do so. This also demands, suitable letter of apology. We should also thank a person for any help he may have extended to us. Courtesy demands that we should correspond through letters on occasions, such as,

- Invitation, ● Sympathy, ● Congratulations, ● Regret Letters,
- Recommendations, ● Obligations, ● Condolence, etc.

(Sample-1)
Griha Pravesh

Dear Deveshji

You would be pleased to know that the 'Griha Pravesh" ceremony of our new house will take place at 10.00 in the morning on Moday dated...

You are cordially invited, along with all the family members to grace this occasion. We hope, you will oblige us with your presence.

Yours truly,
Sanjay Suri
22, Milansar Apartment
Near Piragarhi, Paschim Vihar
New Delhi - 110063

Naming Ceremony

Dear Nareshji,

You would be pleased to know that we have been blessed with the birth of a son recently. To celebrate the occasion, a 'Namkaran function" has been fixed to take place on Friday, dated...at 5.00 in the evening.

Please accept our humble invitation to grace the ceremony and bless the newborn child along with all your family members.

Yours truly,
Avinash Khatri
21, Milansar Apartment
Near Piragarhi, Paschim Vihar
New Delhi - 110063

(Sample-3)
Inauguration of a Hotel

To

Sri/Smt...

Warm greetings!

You would be pleased to know that on the occasion of launching our new hotel 'Samrat", a 'Satyanarayan Puja" has been organised at 11.00 in the morning on Sunday, dated...

On this auspicious occasion, may we request you to kindly visit us along with your family members and close friends, accept the 'prasad" and help us relish the sense of fulfilment.

Yours truly,
Anand Singh

R.S.V.P.
Samrat Hotel
Address:

(Sample-4)

Invitation for Dinner

Dear Sunil Sagarji,

Warm greetings!

You would be pleased to know that my son, Manish has been selected in the IAS.

To celebrate the occasion, we are hosting a dinner at our house at 9.00 in the evening on Sunday, dated…

We hope you would oblige us with your honourable presence.

Yours truly,
Arvind Anand
Address:

(Sample-5)

Felicitation

A warm invitation is extended to
Smt and Sri…
to attend a dinner party hosted on 21 April XX
to honour and felicitate
Smt and Sri Vijay Kumar I.G.
We hope you will kindly honour the invitation.

Yours sincerely,
Devendra Sharma
Address:

Time: 5.00 p.m.
Dress: Formal
R.S.V.P.

(Sample-6)

Felicitation

A warm invitation is extended to
Smt and Sri...
to attend a dinner party hosted at Hotel Janpath on
21/4/XX at 5.00 p.m.
to honour and felicitate
Smt and Sri Vijay Kumar I.G.
We hope you will kindly honour the invitation,
and grace the occasion.

Yours sincerely,
Devendra Sharma
Address:

Hotel Janpath
R.S.V.P.

(Sample-7)

Felicitation

Devendra Sharma cordially invites Smt/Sri... to a dinner function hosted at Hotel Janpath on 21/4/20XX at 5.00 p.m. in the honour of Smt/Sri Vijay Kumar, Inspector General.

I hope you will kindly grace the occasion.

Address
R.S.V.P.

(Sample-8)
(Accepting the Invitation)

Dear Devendra Sharmaji,

It feels nice to receive your invitation card. We will surely attend the function hosted at Hotel Janpath on 21/4/20XX at 5.00 p.m. in the honour of Smt/Sri Vijay Kumar. Being invited to such an august function is a testimony to your dedication and sincerity.

Your friend,
Bhuvanesh Ranjan
Address

Dated...

(Sample-9)
Declining the Invitation

Dear Devendra Sharmaji,

We are truly grateful to you for the courtesy extended to us to join the dinner function hosted in the honour of Smt/Sri Vijay Kumarji, I.G. We regret to inform you that due to ill health of my mother, it will not be possible for us to join you. I hope you will appreciate my inconvenience.

Your friend,
Bhuvanesh Ranjan
Address

Dated...

(Sample-10)

Dinner Invitation

Chaitanya 'Suman" extends an invitation to Smt/Sri…
to attend a dinner being hosted at Hotel Samrath (address)
on 4/3/20XX at 5.00 p.m.
Trust the couple would grace the occasion.

Dated…
Address
R.S.V.P.

(Sample-11)

Smt/Sri…is requested to attend
a dinner being hosted at Hotel Samrath
on 4/3/20XX at 5.00 p.m.

Hotel Samrath
Address
Dated…
R.S.V.P.

(Sample-12)

(Accepting the Invitation)

Dear Sumanji,

Thank you for your kind invitation. Your Bhabhi felt happy when I handed her the invitation. We look forward to partake the dinner at 5.00 p.m. on 4/3/XX.

Yours,
Aman Srivastava
Address

Dated…

(Sample-13)

(Declining the Invitation)

Dear Chaitanyaji,

Thank you for your kind invitation. I really wished to sit with you and relish the dinner. Unfortunately, on 4/3/20XX, I have to go out of town on an urgent work. I hope you will appreciate my inconvenience and would excuse my absence.

Yours,
Aman Srivastava
Address

Dated…

Invitation for Refreshment

Invitation for refreshment is sent in a manner identical to 'dinner". Replies to such invitation are sent on similar lines except that 'refreshment" is written in place of 'dinner".

In India, the concept of lunch, dinner and breakfast is quite different from the one seen in western countries.

It is important to convey acceptance or otherwise of every invitation in a timely manner so as to keep the host informed suitably.

(Sample-1)
Declining the Invitation

Dear friend,

Thank you for your kind invitation. I really wished to sit with you and relish the dinner. Unfortunately, I will not be able to take part because I have already accepted an invitation elsewhere on this particular day. I hope you will appreciate my inconvenience and would excuse my absence.

Yours sincerely,
Ravi Saxena
Address

Dated...

Declining the Invitation

Dear friend,

Your obedient pupil warmly thanks you for your kind invitation for dinner. I regret with heavy heart, to inform you that it will not be possible for me to attend the dinner due to the illness of my wife. I hope you will appreciate my inconvenience and would excuse my absence.

Yours pupil,
Vidya Sagar
Address

Dated...

(Sample-3)
Declining the Invitation

Dear Damini,

Thank you for your kind invitation for dinner. It is a matter of utmost satisfaction to receive one. I imagine, it would have been wonderful to sit with you and enjoy the dinner. I regret to inform you that due to the sickness of my son, I will have to attend to him since there is none to take care. I hope you will appreciate my inconvenience and would excuse my absence.

Your younger brother,
Anant Upadhyay
Address

Dated...

(Sample-4)

Invitation to Participate in a Cultural Programme

Dear Brajeshji,

    I have invited a few of my close friends in the evening of the 25th April, 20XX for dinner. On that day itself, India-fame Yatin Sahani would be performing his new play in the local auditorium. It is my sincere desire that you should spare time to grace the occasion and allow the gathering present therein to enjoy your wit, light jokes and humour. My friends have been pressurising me for quite some time the need for your presence. I hope you will be kind enough to honour the request of my friends.

Yours sincerely,
Jayesh Saxena

Dated...
R.S.V.P.

(Sample-5)

Acceptance of the Invitation

Dear Jayeshji,

    I am grateful for the invitation you have sent to witness the play being performed by India-fame Yatin Sahani in the local auditorium. Likewise, I am truly obliged to be invited to partake the dinner organised, just prior to the start of the play. I hope to enjoy an eventful evening.

Yours sincerely,
Brajesh

Dated...

Declining the Invitation

Dear friend,

I am grateful to you for sending us an invitation to join a tea party followed by witnessing a football match. It is difficult to decline either of the events. Despite this, you can"t always turn away from social obligations. You might be remembering the old lady who stays on the upper floor of my house. She is not keeping well and is critical. Her condition necessitated me to take a day off yesterday. I hope you would appreciate my responsibility and would excuse me for declining the invitation.

Your sincerely,
Anuj Tripathi
Address

Dated...

(Sample-7)
Invitation to a Picnic

Dear Rajni,

We have planned a picnic trip to Surajkund, the coming Sunday. We will be having our lunch there itself. It would be great to have you join us on this occasion. I hope you will accept our invitation.

Your brother,
Narottam Sehgal
Address

Dated...
R.S.V.P.

(Sample-8)
Acceptance of the Invitation

Dear Narottam,

It is a pleasure to receive your invitation to the planned picnic trip to Surajkund, the coming Sunday. It"s enjoyable to go out with Bhabhi and Mataji. I would definitely join you on this occasion. In fact, I would be reaching your place by Saturday evening itself.

Convey my regards to Mataji.

Yours affectionately,
Rajni
Address

Dated...

(Sample-9)
Declining the Invitation

Dear Narottam,

It is a pleasure to receive your invitation for a picnic trip to Surajkund, the coming Sunday. But I regret I will not be able to join you all. Your Jijaji is coming this Sunday along with a few of his friends. I am expected to take care of their convenience. Kindly convey my inability to Mataji to join you all to the picnic.

Yours affectionately,
Rajni
Address

Dated...

(Sample-10)
Invitation to a Show

Dear Dipti,

Popular artist and dancer Sri Surajmal Maharaj is displaying his theatrics at the Kamani Auditorium tomorrow evening. I have already booked two seats. I would like you to join me in enjoying the show. I hope you will reach my house in time.

Yours truly,
Sagar
Address

Dated...
R.S.V.P.

(Sample-11)
Acceptance of the Invitation

Dear Sagar,

It is great to know that world renowned artist and dancer Sri Surajmal Maharaj is displaying his theatrics at the Kamani Auditorium tomorrow evening. Your invitation came as a pleasant surprise to me. I would like to join you in enjoying the show. Be sure, I will reach your house in time.

Yours truly,
Dipti

Address
Dated...

(Sample-12)
Invitation Declined

Dear Sagar,

Thanks for your invitation. It is great to know that world renowned artist and dancer Sri Surajmal Maharaj is displaying his theatrics at the Kamani Auditorium tomorrow evening. I feel extremely sorry to decline your invitation to join you to witness the great dancer in action.

It so happened that my younger brother Bobby slipped from the roof and injured himself badly. We are afraid to move out not knowing when we would be needed. I hope you will excuse me for not joining yo.

Yours truly,
Dipti
Address

Dated...

(Sample-13)

Invitation to a Book Fair

Dear Anushka,

You would be pleased to know that a 7-day Book Fair is being organised at the Pragati Maidan in Delhi. Book publishers from India and abroad would be taking part in this event. I have decided to go to Delhi to visit this book fair. For quite some time, we have not met. I look forward to meeting you during this trip to Delhi.

Yours truly,
Nibhrant
Address

Dated...
R.S.V.P.

(Sample-14)

Acceptance of the Invitation

Dear Nibhrant,

Thank you for your kind invitation to join you to visit the book fair being organised at the Pragati Maidan in Delhi. I have heard a lot about this great event. I too have not been able to meet you for long due to a hectic work schedule. I look forward to visiting the book fair with you in company.

Yours sincerely,
Anushka
Address

Dated...

(Sample-15)

Invitation Declined

Dear Nibhrant,

Thank you for your kind invitation to join you to visit the book fair being organised at the Pragati Maidan in Delhi. I have heard a lot about this great event. But due to the increased workload in the office, I am not able to go home before 8 – 9 in the evening. I hope, next week, I may be able to take a few days break. Under the situation I am in presently, I would like to be excused from visiting the book fair.

Yours sincerely,
Anushka
Address

Dated...

(Sample-16)

Engagement Ceremony

Smt/Sri ...

Is requested to join the tea party organised on 3/3/20XX at 5.00 in the evening at the Shyam Banquet. A small function has been organised to celebrate the auspicious settlement of marriage of Ramesh with Kamlesh Kumari, M.A., daughter of Smt. and Sri Radhika Ramanji of Varanasi. Kindly grace the occasion along with your family members and honour us by your presence.

Humbly Solicited by,
Vijay Sabbarwal

Dated:
R.S.V.P.

(Sample-17)

Acceptance of the Invitation

Dear Sir,

We learnt with pleasure the auspicious settlement of marriage of Ramesh with Kamlesh Kumari, M.A., daughter of Smt. and Sri Radhika Ramanji of Varanasi. We would attend the tea party organised on this occasion.

Yours truly,
Naresh Pathak
Address

Dated:
R.S.V.P.

(Sample-18)
Declining the Invitation

Dear Sir,

Warm greetings! We received your kind invitation and learnt with much delight the auspicious settlement of marriage of your son Ramesh with Kamlesh Kumari, M.A., daughter of Smt. and Sri Radhika Ramanji of Varanasi. Despite our strong desire to join you on this occasion, I am very sad to inform you that I am going to Chandigarh on an urgent assignment. I hope you will excuse my absence.

Yours
Naresh Pathak
Address

Dated:
R.S.V.P.

(Sample-19)
Marriage Invitation Card

!!Shubh Vivah!!
!! Sri Ganeshaya Namah!!
Aniket Singh
S/O Late Surendra Singh
Weds
Sunita Singh
D/O Late Jainendra Singh
On the auspicious and solemn occasion of two souls getting united, kindly bestow on the young couple your choicest blessings and honour us with your gracious presence.

Solicited by :   Requested by
Singh Family   Jai Narayan Singh
                                                              Schedule

Dwarchar: Friday, 29th November, 7.00 Evening
Vivah: Friday, 29th November, 10.00 Evening
Vidai: Saturday, 30th November, 10.00 Morning

!!Venue!!
Navrang Hotel Cantt, Varanasi (UP)

Note: The *barat* party will depart from our village, Niamatganj on Friday, 29th November, 2011 at 12.00 noon by bus and reach Vishal Hotel, Cantt, Varanasi in the evening.

(Sample-20)

I feel honoured to inform Smt/Sri …that by the grace of God, the marriage of my son Suresh Khatri with Kavya Kumari, (D/O Smt/Sri Hari Nath Khatri of Bareilly) is fixed to be solemnised on the auspicious day of 9/9/20XX. You are humbly requested to bless the young couple.

Yours sincerely,
Ramdas Khatri

B-278, Ekta Apartment
Pashchim Vihar
New Delhi – 110063
R.S.V.P.

(Sample-21)

I feel honoured to inform Smt/Sri …that by the grace of God, the marriage of my younger brother Shiv Narain with Renu (D/O Sri Raja Ramji of Agra) is fixed to be solemnised on the auspicious day of 2.11/20XX. Please honour us, along with your children and grace the occasion by blessingt he young couple. The *barat* will leave by bus in the morning of 2/11/20XX.

Yours,
Krishna Nath Shastri

234, Gali Mirabai
Delhi - 110006
R.S.V.P.

I feel honoured to inform Smt/Sri … that by the grace of God, the marriage of my son Anoop Singh with Shobna (D/O Sri Roop Narain Ji of Bareilly) is fixed to be solemnised on the auspicious day of 3/2/20XX. Please honour us, along with your children and grace the occasion as per the itinerary given in the invitation card.

(Barat will leave by train at 10.00 in the night of 2/2/20XX)

Yours truly,
Arjun Singh
Address

Dated…
R.S.V.P.

(Sample-23)

Invitation Accepted

Dear Arjunji!

We learnt with pleasure the news of the marriage of your son Anoop Singh with Shobna, D/O Sri Roop Narain Ji of Bareilly to be solemnised on the auspicious day of 3/2/20XX. We will definitely visit and bestow my blessings to Anoop. I had always looked forward to see this occasion fructify at the earliest.

Yours sincerely,
Kamal Kishore
Address

Dated…

(Sample-24)
(Sample-24)
Invitation Declined

Dear Arjunji!

    We learnt with pleasure the news of the marriage of your son Anoop Singh with Shobna, D/O Sri Roop Narain Ji of Bareilly to be solemnised on the auspicious day of 3/2/20XX. I had always looked forward to see this occasion fructify at the earliest. I regret I will not be able to be with you. The reason is somewhat disappointing and hence, I am not mentioning this at the moment. I am sending my best wishes for the young couple. I wish all the best for this marriage..

Yours truly,
Kamal Kishore
Address

Dated…

(Sample-25)
Postponement of Marriage

We regret to announce the marriage of Kumari Archana with Rakesh Kumar scheduled for 23rd June, 2012 has been postponed. Ashish, the younger brother of Archana met with an accident and expired. You will be informed in time as soon as a fresh date of marriage is finalised. We beg forgiveness for the unintended inconvenience.

Dated:

Vishwa Mohan
Address

Letters Sent Post-marriage

It is an Indian tradition that the bridegroom side presents gifts to the bride. This is usually given the name of 'Muh Dikhai". A letter conveying acceptance of the gift goes a long way in cementing the relationship.

This kind of letter is ordinarily written in the following way.

Dear Sadanandji!

It was very kind of you to have presented me a gift, which I very graciously accept. This is an invaluable presentation. I very much look forward to meet you in person in this new house of mine.

Yours truly,
Kanchan Kumari
Address

(Sample-27)

Dear Sir!

It"s kind of you to have thought of me to be deserving such a precious gift. It was really an honour. I look forward to meet you as a hostess of this new house of mine. I hope such an occasion would come soon.

Yours truly,
Kanchan Kumari
Address

Arranging a Tea Party to Introduce the Newlywed Couple

Smt. and Sri...are kindly requested to grace a tea-party organised at 'Sona & Roopa Restaurant" tomorrow dated 3rd February, 20XX at 5.00 in the evening. The party is intended to introduce Smt. Kavita Tilak, the newlywed wife of my bosom friend, Sri Ajay Tilakji among our close circle. We hope you would graciously join the function.

Dated:

Dinesh Kumar
Address

Acceptance of the Above

Dear Dineshji!

It is with pleasure that I received your invitation to attend a tea party to introduce Smt Kavita Tilak, the newlywed wife of Sri Ajay Tilakji among our close circle. I really felt honoured by this. At the appointed time, I would be there at Sona and Roopa restaurant to bless the young couple.

Dinesh Kumar
Address

Dated...

(Sample-30)
Declining the Above

Dear Dineshji!

It is with pleasure I received your invitation to attend a tea party to introduce Smt Kavita Tilak, the newlywed wife of Sri Ajay Tilakji among our close circle. I really felt honoured by this. I regert it will not be possible for me to attend the function since I am suffering from fever for the last four days.

I hope you will appreciate my inconvenience and excuse me.

Kindly bless the young couple on my behalf.

Your friend,
Rohit
Address

Dated…

(Sample-31)
Invitation on the Occasion of Birthday

Sri/Smt…Ji

By the grace of God, a baby boy was born to my son Anmol. On this occasion, a dinner party has been hosted at 6.00 in the evening on 19.2.20XX at my house. I hope to have the pleasure of having you to celebrate the birth of the boy.

Yours sincerely,
Gopal Mishra
Address

Dated…

Accepting the Above Invitation

Dear Mishraji,

We all felt thrilled to hear the news of the birth of a baby boy to Anmol. God has bestowed an invaluable delight in the life of Anmol. God has also showered you a favour by granting your wish for which you had waited so long.

I will find time soon to be with you all.

Your loving brother,
Amit Mishra
Address

Dated…

(Sample-33)
Declining the Above Invitation

Dear Mishraji,

We received the invitation sent in the name of my parents. It was thrilling to hear the news of the birth of a baby boy to Anmol. It will not be possible for my parents to join you on this occasion since they have gone abroad on 8.2.20XX for about a month. I am conveying this news to them today itself.

On behalf of my parents and myself, please accept our best wishes.

Your younger daughter,
Rajni
Address

Dated…

(Sample-34)
Invitation for Mundan Ceremony

Sri/Smt ...Ji!

Ankur has completed two years and is stepping into his third year of life on Wednesday, 22.2.20XX. On this occasion, we have decided to organise a Mundan ceremony according to our Yagya Vidhi. Thereafter, dinner has also been scheduled.

Kindly make it convenient to bless the child.

Yours truly,
Saurabh Sharma
Address

Dated...

(Sample-35)

Acceptance of the Invitation for Mundan Ceremony

Dear Saurabhji!

The moment we received the invitation regarding Ankur"s second birthday and the coming Mundan ceremony, the memory of the invitation on his first birthday flashed across our minds vividly. That time he was lying on a swing and giving out gurgling smiles. I will surely join you on this occasion.

Yours truly,
Prem Prakash
Address

Dated...

(Sample-36)
Declining the Invitation for Mundan Ceremony

Dear Saurabhji!

We received your invitation. That Ankur has completed two years and is moving into the third is a matter of great rejoice for all of us. We hope he keeps hale and hearty all through. We wanted to actively participate in the Mundan ceremony but for some unforeseen circumstances, it is just not possible to make a visit. We are sending our best wishes to Ankur.

Yours sincerely,
Prem Prakash
Address

Dated…

(Sample-37)
Invitation on the Death of Father

Dear friend,

It is with a heavy heart, I have to inform you that my father left for his heavenly abode this morning at 5.35. I have lost him forever. I am totally shocked what to do. Now, it"s you and other close friends who will guide me in this difficult hour. I have decided to open a library in the name of my father. The *Rasam Pagdi* has been planned for 3.2.20XX. Kindly guide me and be with me in this hour of distress.

Yours sincerely,
Vinay Kumar
Address

Dated…

(Sample-38)
Accepting the Above Invitation

Dear Vinay,

The sad news of the death of my Bhaiyya sent a shock wave through all of us here. Your *chachi* always regarded him as her elder brother. Tonight itself, I am catching a train to reach you. You are wise and intelligent and know how to conduct yourself in difficult circumstances. I hope you will bravely negotiate this difficult time. Please don"t despair. It"s time for you to console others. Be brave.

Your Uncle,
Suryamani
Address

Dated…

(Sample-39)
Declining the Above Invitation

Dear Vinay,

The sad news of the death of your father sent a shock wave through all of us here. Heavy responsibility has fallen on your shoulder to console your bereaving family members and keep them intact. I regret, in the absence of my doctor"s advice, I can"t really take a chance to move out. I am sending your sister by train this evening itself. I will reach you as soon as I am in a position to move comfortably.

Yours truly,
Sheel Kumar
Address

Dated…

6

Letters of Sympathy

There are times when a person gets dejected, feels let down and doesn"t quite know what to do – not necessarily due to his fault, mistake or error of judgement. These are the times – hard times- when he yearns for words of sympathy and emotional support. It becomes the moral duty of friends and family members to go out and extend all possible assistance to prevent further deterioration in his mental outlook. A few examples of letters are written below.

(Sample-1)
A Letter of Sympathy

Address of the sender
Dated:

Dear Brother Ramesh,

Namaskar,

Today"s newspaper carried results the of your examination. I felt disappointed at not finding your name.

I need not mention that you must have felt the shock in equal measure, if not more. But then, please realise that life is composed of both ups and downs. Life goes on. It doesn"t stop. You have to get up, dust yourself and get going. This year, in particular, you didn"t keep good health, and lost three months due to sickness.

One suggestion though! If you are a little tired of Delhi at the moment, why don"t you come over to Shimla and spend some time here in altogether new surroundings away from the hustle and bustle of traffic, speed and noise. Your Bhabhi remembers you very much. Your nephew Kunnu also longs to be near you. He would be a plaything for you while keeping you company.

Yours affectionately,
Suresh

(Reply to the Above)

Address of the sender
Dated:

Dear Brother,
Namaskar,

I am in receipt of your letter. No doubt, I failed but I am not the sort of person to lay prostrate in front of the failure. During three months of my sickness, I have completely revised the syllabus but then the culprit, 'sickness" didn"t spare me.

Well! Whatever had to happen has happened. The plain fact is I am quite sick of the environment here. I am catching a train tomorrow to reach you. In the good company of children and Bhabhiji, I will be able to divert my attention and move on in life.

Please convey my regards to Bhabhiji and love to children.

Yours affectionately,
Ramesh

(Sample-2)

On Losing a Football Match at School

Address of the sender
Dated:

Dear Baldev,

I have come to know that our school team lost in the final of the football match by a slender goal. That apart, I am also told that your all-round display had sent shivers down the spine of the rival team. What I would like to stress is that this loss should cause you no worry and that such occasions keep cropping up every now and then. But the life goes on unmindful of what happened yesterday.

I regret I couldn"t take the field due to my illness, but am proud of your field management.

What significantly matters is, not the loss in the final, but the manner in which you carried the day, which in effect, translates into your personal victory.

I hope you are not disappointed; and will look forward to leading the team with renewed vigour and vitality.

Your friend,
Raj

(Reply)

Address of the sender
Dated:

Dear Raj,

I received your letter. In your absence, it was very difficult to manage the show, but then we tried our best to take every match unitedly. We went right up to the final. Unfortunately, during the final match, my ankle twisted and the ball slipped through me into the goal line.

Now, we are focussing on the tournaments coming ahead. I hope, very soon, you will be joining us. Your absence has really handicapped us. Get well soon and join us to take our team ahead. God willing!

Your friend,
Baldev

(Sample-3)

Being Unsuccessful at a Competitive Examination

Address
Dated…

Dear Rajan,

I got a letter from Jeetendra this afternoon. It informed me of your failure to crack the examination held for the job. There is nothing to feel disheartened about. Success and failure are part of everyone"s life.

There is no point in rejoicing at success or showing despair at failure.

Initially, I could scarcely believe you were writing any competitive examination. I feel sure, this disappointment won"t hamper your ambition and would, in fact, propel you to constantly strive to move ahead in life.

Your friend,
Vinay

(Reply)

Address
Dated…

Dear Vinay,

I am in receipt of your letter. I am surely disappointed for failing to succeed at the examinations, but then I realise things like these go on. Your letter brought some solace, and comfort to me. In circumstances, such as this, only someone very close to you can fathom your feelings and touch the chord.

I know one day I would succeed.

Rest all is fine.

Your friend,
Rajan

(Sample -4)

Letter from a Father to his Son who has Lost his Job

Address
Dated…

My dear son,

Your mother tells me that by a letter, your wife has informed that for some unforeseen reason, you have been removed from the job. I can very well understand the sense of despondency you must be undergoing at the moment. But remember, life consists of both good and no-so-good times. The one who faces them squarely is the ultimate winner.

You are a son of a fearless father who has never bowed before any circumstances. I feel sure you would also come out unscathed. You have a solid character and I hope you will do nothing to impair that. Meanwhile, please come over to us for a change. In the meantime, we will try to get in touch with your senior officials to investigate the cause of your removal. Have no sense of fear or guilt.

Please come home soon.

Your father,
Vishwa Mohan

(Reply)

My dear father,

Your letter gave me a sense of comfort and well-being that I had lost for the past one week. That I lost the job is of little consequence, but what hurts me is my honesty, which was overlooked. Circumstances that floated before me could have made me millions, but my mind didn"t let me proceed. The result is there for you and I to see.

For quite some time, various kinds of insinuations and jibes were thrown at me but all of them remained unsuccessful. It was becoming increasingly difficult for me to adjust to the environment that prevailed here.

I have collected enough evidence to back my case. I have already written to the minister as well as to the secretary. They have assured me of looking into the case expeditiously. In case, nothing works, courts are the ultimate weapon of sorts. I am coming soon to discuss things over with you.

Your loving son,
Naresh

(Sample-5)

Factory Destroyed in Fire

Address
Dated…

Dear Pradeep,

It was highly disturbing to read in the newspaper the spate of fires occurring in factories in Delhi. It was emotionally painful to learn that your factory was also gutted in the inferno. I could scarcely visualise the memories of the large factory you had built.

The factory lives today in all, but memory and imagination. Nevertheless, I am sure, like the previous occasions where you had overcome many setbacks in the course of your business, you would succeed in rebuilding a still larger factory.

Please don"t hesitate to call me if you consider me worthy of any contribution.

Your friend,
Atma Dev

(Reply)

Address
Dated...

Dear Atma Devji!

    I have received your emotionally charged letter today. You have lent me a crucial support at this juncture which will go a long way in lowering my difficulties. The fire was a real inferno that engulfed shops after shops in a large area. Along with mine, four other factories went into the flames completely. More than 500 workers lost their jobs and properties worth crores were destroyed by the fire.

    Very few come forward to stand at times of real need. I won"t forget your strong feelings for me.

    God is great. Nothing stands invincible before Him.

    We have to learn to live with Him.

Your friend,
Pradeep

(Sample-6)

On Losing an Election

Address
Dated...

Dear Jai Prakashji!

    I was painful to hear of the election result of your constituency. It is a matter of regret that the voters have chosen to send your rival Sri Ram Dayal Ji to parliament as their representative instead of a genuine worker like yourself. Except for raising his hand in support or otherwise of any issue, he would hardly do anything else.

    The voters are illiterate and because of this, they send representatives like Sri Ram Dayal Ji. It matters little for dedicated people like you to officially represent any constituency. Work is worship for you. I am sure you would hardly care for this result.

Yours sincerely,
Ramanuj

(Reply)

Address
Dated…

Dear Ramanujji!

I received your letter of sympathy. Winning or losing are just the two possible outcomes of any election. If not a victory, losing is the only alternative. I wanted to go to parliament for a certain cause.

I would have represented that cause in particular. I am a dedicated soldier and am not afraid of anything.

I know many more such occasions would come in future. I know I can rely on friends like you.

Yours sincerely,
Jai Prakash

(Sample-7)

On Being Attacked

Address
Dated…

Dear Suryabhanji!

Just now I learnt from Atmanand that some miscreants attacked you at night the day before yesterday due to which you suffered injuries in your hands and legs. It was quite painful to hear this dastardly attack. I guess these people are the same with whom you have a long running court case. It is shocking that they attacked a person while asleep.

If there is anything I could do, please don"t hesitate to call me. I would immediately rush. Right now, I couldn"t make it to you because my son is very ill. I would reach you as soon as he recovers from his illness.

Yours,
Jai Prakash

(Reply)

Address
Dated...

Dear Raghunandanji!

I received your letter just now. I have received letters of sympathy from all those who heard this. Anyway, whatever had to happen has happened. Nothing could be done about this. You may be pleased to know that I fought four of the miscreants single-handedly. You may be right in guessing that these hired goons were sent by the person with whom I have an account case running for long.

I have not really suffered much. Kindly convey my regards to Bhabhiji and inform her that there is nothing to worry. I thank you for enquiring about my welfare.

If there is anything I could do, please don"t hesitate to call me. I would immediately rush and be at your service at the earliest.

Yours,
Suryabhan

(Sample-8)

Theft in the House

Address
Dated...

Dear Jijaji!

I received the sad news through Didi"s letter just now. I was stunned to hear of the theft committed in the house. For a moment, I failed to apprehend what"s happened.

Jija Ji, you are elder to me, so for me to discourse you on patience and forbearance looks inappropriate. Nevertheless, to regret what has already been done makes little justice and a waste of time.

Please don"t hesitate to ask me to do anything you believe I am capable of as I am always ready. I am leaving by train tomorrow to reach you. Kindly console Didi on this unfortunate account.

Yours,
Kumar

(Sample-9)

On Losing an Election

Address
Dated…

Dear Harsh!

I came to know through Surendra Mohan that you have lost the court case. It"s very painful. But then, the brave never fear the loss and remain unperturbed. I am sure this loss will not have much effect on you. You have won as well as lost umpteen cases like this one. I am of the opinion that you should file a case in the Supreme Court. It"s quite possible; the lower court"s decision could be set aside. From my side, I would strive hard to use my resources to the maximum possible extent. Please try to get over this loss.

Yours sincerely,
Shashibhushan

(Reply to the Above)

Address
Dated…

Dear Shashibhushan!

I received your letter and felt quite relieved. This particular case consumed three precious years. And the outcome was zero. The matter stayed where it was. Time, money and energy all gone down the drain.

What I am really worried is not the loss of money, time or energy but the honour and name and fame. I will consider your opinion and appeal in the Supreme Court. Let"s see the outcome there. Our job is to do our bit and hope for the best. I am coming to Delhi to offer my support and guidance.

Your younger brother,
Harsh

(Sample-10)

On the Death of a Close Relative

Address
Dated…

Dear Purushottam Prasadji!

It was painful to hear from Jeevan Lal Ji that your brother Sri Dushyant Ji expired at 12 in the afternoon yesterday. It is an irreparable loss to your family. It is difficult to recount the number of occasions Dushyant Ji had pulled the family out of hard times. In fact, you never really had to worry as long as he was alive. Now the responsibility squarely rests on your head. I hope you will do your best as far as taking care of them is concerned.

Please don"t hesitate to call me for whatever worth you consider me. May God help him rest in peace and allow Bhabhiji and her children to forebear the loss.

Your friend,
Rajpal

(Reply to the Above)

Address
Dated…

Dear Rajpal!

I am grateful to you for sending me your sympathies. The untimely demise of my dear brother has really sucked the strength out of me. While he was alive, I was having a smooth and uninterrupted life. He was shouldering the complete responsibility of the family. I was never required to worry about anything.

Now suddenly, the responsibility has fallen on my shoulders. I hope he will continue to guide us from where he resides in heaven. I am sure, with people like you around, I will have every kind of support whenever needed.

I have not been able to send a prompt and coherent reply due to my current state of mind. I hope you will forgive me for this.

Your friend,
Purushottam Prasad

Congratulatory Letters

Occasions arise when we feel like congratulating someone on achieving something remarkable.

Given below are a few examples of messages sent on different occasions.

(Sample-1)

Congratulatory Letter on the Publication of a Magazine

Name and address of the sender
Date...

Dear Dr.Vaibhavji,

Hearty congratulations!

I received you letter and learnt of the successful publication of the magazine, 'Jan Bharti". As I was out of town, I regret that I couldn"t reply earlier.

I wish you all the best in your farsighted effort in publishing a magazine that reflects the current thoughts on literature, culture and the national ideals. Please accept my wishes once again!

Regards,

Yours affectionately,
Prem Prakash

Congratulating a Friend on Topping the B.A. Exams and Getting Honoured with Gold Medal

Dear Ravi,

Many congratulations!

It was pleasure no end for me on learning that not just the college, you have topped the Mumbai University in the recently held B.A. examinations. That Mumbai University chose to honour you with the Gold Medal has sent me soaring into the seventh heaven. I am short of words and just don"t know how to express my heart-felt emotions. Please accept my best wishes! It was made possible because of your single-handed effort and devotion; apart from your equally sound activities at games and sports.

I strongly feel that likewise you will achieve an identical result in your M.A. examinations and make your parents proud. I wish you continue on this path of success in all your future endeavours. My parents are sending their best wishes for you.

Please convey my regards to your parents and love to your younger brother, Rohan.

Yours affectionately,
Manoj

(Sample-3)

Congratulating a Friend on Getting a Ph.D Degree

Name and address of the sender
Dated...

Dear Vijaykantji,

Warm greetings!

It gave me immense pleasure to learn that the Delhi University has honoured you with the degree of a Ph.D (Name of the subject). My sincere congratulations to you on this remarkable achievement!

I wish you achieve innumerable such successes in life!

Yours truly,
Narendra Rajput

(Sample-4)
Greeting on the Birthday of a Friend

Name and address of the sender
Dated…

Dear Ashok,

Warm greetings!

I received your birthday invitation card. Thank you for the same. I always grow impatient for your birthday as soon as January gets near. It is nearly impossible to forget birthdays of friends like you.

I am afraid I will not be able to join the birthday celebrations this time because my mother is due for an eye operation. There is none to take care of her. In case, my father gets leave from the office, I would certainly join you all.

I wish, every moment of life bestows you happiness and pleasure. On your birthday, I am sending you a few books on literature and a camera. I hope you will like them.

Congratulations from my side again.

Please convey my regards to your parents and love to youngsters.

Best wishes!

Your friend,
Vijayendra

(Sample-5)
Congratulatory Letter on Winning an Election

Name and address of the sender
Dated…

Dear Swaroopchandji,

Warm greetings!

Congratulations on winning the seat in the Uttar Pradesh Vidhan Sabha election by the highest margin.

I hope the condition prevailing in the State will improve and the development works taken in the right earnest.

Yours truly,
Devesh

(Sample-6)
Congratulatory Letter on Being Appointed as a Lecturer

Name and address of the sender
Dated…

Dear Rajesh,

Warm greetings!

I received your letter today. It gave me a great pleasure to learn that you have been appointed as a lecturer in English in the prestigious Pune"s College of Arts and Commerce. My parents felt hugely exhilarated on hearing this news. Congratulations once again!

Please treat the students in a friendly manner. Your sincerity will take you a long way in pursuit of a great career.

Yours truly,
Anand Kumar

(Sample-7)
Congratulations on Winning a Lottery

Name and address of the sender
Dated…

Dear Jayant,

Your family members informed me that you have won a lottery for ₹ 10 lakh last week. Initially, it was hard to believe, but when your mother showed me your letter regarding this, then I was able to believe. Congratulations to you again!

Now I realise that it is possible to win a dream by spending a rupee or two. I had heard about lottery winners before, but it"s the first time someone close to me has actually won it. I have also come to believe that lotteries are run fairly.

Goddess Lakshmi bestows her rewards to honest people like you only. You may have seen many people going bust in search of becoming a *lakhpati* by any means- fair or foul.

I hope after taking care of your household, you would contribute some of the amount towards the national fund for earthquake victims.

Everyone here is fine. Convey my regards to Bhabhiji and love to Armaan.

Yours sincerely,
Akash

(Sample-8)

Congratulations on the Birth of a Baby Boy/Girl

Name and address of the sender
Dated…

Dear Bhabhiji,

Ramesh bhaiyya informed us that you have given birth to a baby boy. We felt overjoyed with this news. Ammaji and Babuji are also extremely happy. Many congratulations to you and the young one! My mother is quite anxious to see the baby.

Kindly pay our regards to your parents and love to the youngsters in the family. This Sunday, I am coming there along with my mother.

Rest all is fine.

Yours affectionately,
Sachin

(Sample-9)

Congratulations on the Publication of a Novel

Name and address of the sender
Dated…

Dear Sagarji,

I received your letter dated… I couldn"t reply earlier because of certain important engagement. It"s a matter of pleasure that your novel, 'Arunima" has come out of print.

Your contribution for the literature, culture and national integration is truly worthwhile and appreciable.

Kindly accept my congratulations once again.

Yours sincerely,
Utkarsh Tiwari

(Sample-10)

Congratulations on Being Appointed as a Special Executive Officer

Name and address of the sender

Dated...

Dear Swadeshji,

It is a great news to hear that the Delhi government has appointed you as a Special Executive Officer. Congratulations on this happy news.

I hope you are keeping well.

Yours sincerely,

Sagar Sinha

(Sample-11)

Forms of Greetings on Diwali

Best wishes on the auspicious occasion of Diwali!
May you live your life like the glittering festival of Diwali, happy healthy and wealthy!
A Very Very Happy Diwali!
Diwali night is full of lights, may your life be filled with colours and lights of happiness.
Happy Diwali!
May this Diwali be as bright as ever!
May this Diwali bring joy, health and prosperity to you!
May the festival of lights brighten you and your near and dear ones" lives!
May this Diwali bring in you the brightest and choicest happiness and love you have ever wished for!
May this Diwali bring you the utmost in peace and prosperity!
May lights triumph over darkness!
May the spirit of light illuminate your world!
May the light that we celebrate at Diwali show us the way and lead us together on the path of peace and social harmony!
'WISH YOU A VERY HAPPY DIWALI"!

(Sample-12)

New Year Greetings

Here comes the new ones that will bring you cheer; Forget the past, the future is here; Let us welcome the Happy New Year!

Sending you the warmest hugs of the season… and wishing you the best of times. Happy New Year!

So many ways to greet you Happy New Year, but I reserve the most special one to you. I love you anytime of the year.
Happy New Year!

Each moment in a day has its own value. Morning brings HOPE, Afternoon brings FAITH, Evening brings LOVE, Night brings REST, Hope you will have all of them every day. HAPPY NEW YEAR!

A New Year starts, with a new calendar. But my love stays constant, with you always in my heart. Happy New Year!

Wishing you all the blessings of the New Year...the warmth of home, the love of family and the company of good friends!
Happy New Year to all!

Let us greet the New Year with the hope that it will be a better year for all of us!
Happy New Year!

May God continue to bless you and your family with the divine light, love and power that will bring much love, joy, peace, inner strength and overflowing abundance in your home!
Happy New Year!

A blessed & joyous New Year to you and your family!

May the Goddess continue to bless you and your family with the things that matter most in life - a gift of good health, happy home and peace of mind throughout the coming year!
Happy New Year!

12 months have passed, and another 12 will come, but my memory of you remains constant in my mind. Happy New Year my love!

Sunrise makes our mornings beautiful and makes our lives more meaningful.
Happy New Year!

Keep the smile, Leave the tear, Think of joy, Forget the fear, Hold the laugh, Leave the pain, Be joyous! Because it"s New Year!
Happy New Year!

(Sample-13)
Birthday Greetings

Warm wishes on your birthday!
Many happy returns of the day! Happy Birthday!
You will soon start a new phase of life! But that can wait until you are older. Enjoy
another year of being young.
Happy Birthday!
I hope that today is the beginning of a great year for you.
Happy Birthday!
Happy Birthday! Have a wonderful happy, healthy birthday and
many more to come.
You have a birthday twinkle in your eye so have fun and know we
love you fairly much.
Happy Birthday!
Things I like about you: humour, looks, everything.
Happy Birthday!
I love celebrating with you. Thanks for having a birthday and giving us a reason.
Happy Birthday!
I wish you a great and wonderful Happy Birthday!! I hope you have an amazing day
and lots of fun! Enjoy this day, you deserve it!
Hope your day is simply terrific!
Happy Birthday!
Wishing you a spectacularly beautiful birthday!
Happy Birthday!
Wishing you tons of happiness on your birthday!
Enjoy it!
Wishing you love and happiness on your birthday!
Happy Birthday!

(Sample-14)

Responding to a Congratulatory Message

Address:
Dated:

Dear Jijaji,

Saadar Pranam!

Many thanks for the mail and the parcel. I was simply delighted to see the gift.

I just fail to understand, how to reciprocate your feelings of love.

You know for sure my love for photography. The look of the wrist watch and camera are beyond words. I am getting used to wearing this watch and constantly looking for time. The camera is a world unto itself- great to capture images of tourist spots, birthday snaps, etc. I will be able to preserve memories for long with the help of the camera.

I once again thank you for the superb gifts you have sent me. Convey my regards to Didiji and love to Armaan, Muskan and Naisha.

Yours affectionately,
Shubham

Regret Letters

(Sample-1)

Regretting Failure to Submit an Article for the Magazine

Name and address of the sender
Dated:

Dear Shiv Mohanji,

I am grateful to you for your mail. It gives me a great pleasure to learn that you are about to bring out the second edition of the magazine, 'Sahitya Agraj".

Please accept my best wishes.

I regret I am unable to contribute any article due to my hectic schedule and my failing health.

I hope you will accept my apology.

Thanking you,

Yours sincerely,
Sooraj Prakash

(Sample-2)
Inability to Attend a Marriage Function

Name and address of the sender
Dated:

Dear Kartikeya,

Thank you for the card inviting me to attend the marriage function. My warmest greetings on the occasion of marriage!

Actually, I had a great desire to attend the function and believed that it would offer me an opportunity to meet my friends of many years.

I regret the marriage day clashed with the date my father was scheduled to undergo a bypass surgery. My presence at the hospital was necessitated all the more because I am the lone child of my parents and there"s none to take care of.

Despite my longing to be with you, it just couldn"t materialise. You understand the predicament I was in at that time.

I am looking forward to meet you and my dear Bhabhi at the first opportunity that comes my way. Please convey my regards to Bhabhi and respect to the elders and love to all the young ones in the family.

I trust you all are keeping well.

Your friend,
Yogesh

(Sample-3)
Seeking Excuse for Not Reaching on the Demise of Friend"s Father

Name and address of the sender
Dated:

Dear Bhupendra,

I received the painful news of the sad demise of your father. He was loved by one and all. Living for others seemed to be his motto. I don"t remember ever seeing him in a furious mood.

I wanted to take part in the last rites but simply couldn"t do so because my son fell ill around the same time. I hope you will forgive me for this absence.

I will surely be there on the Terahvi".

Your friend,

Rakesh

(Sample-4)
Seeking Excuse for Not Reaching the Kavya Sammelan

Name and address of the sender
Dated:

Dear Siddhant,

I regret to inform you that on…, I will not be able to reach Kamani Auditorium at witness you reciting poems during the Kavya Sammelan. The reason being that on date day itself, I have to go out of an official work.

I hope you will be kind enough to excuse me.

Your friend,
Abhinandan

(Sample-5)
Letter to Father Seeking Excuse for Falling into Bad Company

Name and address of the sender
Dated:

Dear father,

I understand you have received a letter from our principal. It must have been painful to you. Through this letter, I want to clarify the issue.

Please understand that prior to the incident; I was unaware that Dinesh and Nitin undulge in petty thefts from shops. Last Saturday, they asked me to accompany them to the lake. I agreed. Pretending some urgent work, Dinesh didn"t come along for boating. Nitin and I enjoyed about half an hour of boating in the lake. While returning, Nitin went and sat in a taxi. I felt uncomfortable when the taxi started moving towards Kathgodam. On being asked, they said we will go to Delhi. I couldn"t do anything but upon reaching Kathgodam, I made an excuse to call on the nature, I got down, took a lift from a tourist and returned back to Nainital.

Around midnight, I informed the hostel warden who later informed the police. Next day, the police arrested them in Delhi. I beg your forgiveness for my foolishness to be their friends. It won"t happen again in life.

Kindly forgive me and give another chance.

Regards,

Your loving son,
Sarthak Kumar

Letter of Recommendation

(Sample-1)

Introducing a Friend to a Publisher for Publishing his/her Manuscript

Dear Anujji,

I trust this finds you in cheers. For quite some time, I have not received your letter. You are an old hat at not writing letters, nevertheless, there wouldn"t be any disaster, if you write one once in a while.

Sudhanshu Ji who is before you is an old friend of mine – very close, very intimate. He is well versed and equally adept both in writing poems and prose. A number of his books have been published.

Right at the moment, he has approached you with a manuscript – a novel. It has critically analysed the burning problems razing the society currently.

I hope and wish, you will publish his work that he has penned with great diligence.

Yours sincerely,
Vinayak
Address

Dated:

(Affirmative Reply to the Above)

Dear Vinayakji,

Sudhanshuji has handed over your letter to me. I have received the Novel. These days we are not publishing novels but since it"s your wish, we will publish the same.

I regret the delay in replying in time.

Yours friend,
Anuj
Address

Dated…

(Letter of Regret)

Dear Vinayakji,

Sudhanshuji has handed over your letter to me. It would have been pleasing if we could publish the same. Since the last month, my elder brother has taken charge of the publication business. I am in charge of only the press section.

I hope you will appreciate the inconvenience I am feeling in not honouring your word and excuse me for the same.

Rest all is fine.

Yours friend,
Anuj
Address

Dated...

(Sample-2)
Recommending a Known Person for a Job

Dear Prabhakar,

It was pleasing to hear from a machineman, Shyam Singh that your Mansarovar Press is one of the best known presses in Delhi. Shyam Singh is the person carrying this letter to you. He is a dedicated person and is highly duty-bound. He just keeps himself to the job at hand and doesn"t waste time in anything else.

Shyam Singh has worked for us for nearly seven years. During this period, he never gave any opportunity for any complaint. I have come to know that there is a vacancy for a suitable machineman in your press. If you need such a dedicated person, you may hire him.

Please write to me if there is anything I could do for you.

Yours friend,
Virendra
Address

Dated...

(Affirmative Response)

Dear Virendra,

Shyam Singh has given me your letter. What you have written about the successful running of the press is due to well-wishers like you only. A few days ago, I have installed two new presses and for that I need two competent people. In this respect, I had inserted advertisements in *The Times of India* and *Hindustan Times*.

I am already aware of the ability of Shyam Singh. I am much impressed with the books printed in your press. You have greatly eased my problem by recommending an outstanding worker to me.

I have hired Shyam Singh at a salary of ₹ 8,000 per month.

Do let me know if there is anything worthwhile for me to do.

Yours friend,
Prabhakar
Address

Dated…

(Negative Response)

Dear Virendra,

Shyam Singh has given me your letter. The successful running of my press is due to well-wishers like you only. This month I have installed two new presses and for that I needed two competent people. In this respect, I had inserted advertisements in *The Times of India* and *Hindustan Times*. In response, I have only yesterday appointed two machine men.

I wish Shyam Singh had come with your letter yesterday. It would have been my pleasure in appointing him. I feel extremely sorry in not being able to carry out your recommendation. However, I have requested Shyam Singh to keep in touch with me. One never knows when opportunity strikes.

Do let me know if there is anything worthwhile for me to do.

Yours friend,
Prabhakar
Address

Dated…

Recommending a Suitable Person for a Job

Dear Sri Omkar Nathji,

I have come to know that you are working towards opening an NGO (Non-government Organisation) in Bareilly and are in search of a dedicated person to run it efficiently.

A few days back, one of my close friends, Chitraguptaji had come from Benares. He is one of the gems who has dedicated his services for the cause of the society. During discussions with him, I gathered that he is looking out for a base to further the areas of social activities to reach across more needy persons. I believe, if he joins hands with you, his services will help you serve people the way you cherish.

Chitraguptaji is a person, our nation should be proud of. Sincerity, sense of dedication and diligence are the hallmark of his life.

You have adequate funds at your disposal. If he gets a chance to join you, the society will be immensely benefitted.

Kindly inform me by the return of mail, if I should extend him the proposal.

Yours friend,
Som Dutt Narayan
Address

Dated...

(Affirmative Reply to the Above)

Dear Som Duttji,

I have received your mail. By informing me about Chitraguptaji and his ability to run the NGO, you have taken a huge load off my back. I have already opened the NGO, but lack of suitable persons to run it efficiently continues to worry me. I warmly welcome your suggestion. And hope you will promptly invite Chandraguptaji at the earliest so that the job could be entrusted to him.

I would be ever grateful to you for this act.

Yours friend,
Omkar Nath
Address

Dated...

(Negative Reply)

Dear Som Duttji,

I have received your mail. I have no reason to doubt your opinion about Chitraguptaji. But I regret, I am not in a position to assign work to him at the moment. Currently, Brahmachari Sadanandji is efficiently running the job. You would be pleased to know that within a short time, he has been able to do a lot.

I hope this letter keeps you informed and that it won"t be a source of inconvenience to you.

Yours friend,
Omkar Nath
Address

Dated...

Letters Expressing Obligation

Often times, we feel obliged to express our gratitude to someone – friends, relatives, high functionaries or some individuals- for their actions that has helped us in one or more ways. Such letters fall under the heading *individual or public obligatory letters.*

(Sample-1)
Letter Expressing Obligation to an Individual

Name and address of the sender
Dated:

Dear Sir,

Warm greetings!

I am delighted to hear that my son Abhinav has topped his class. I agree he is intelligent and dedicated but I singularly attribute his success to your style and method of teaching. That he would gain immensely under your guidance was something I was pretty sure right from the beginning.

I am heavily indebted to you for the confidence you have reposed in him and placed him where he is today.

I am immensely grateful to you.

Please accept my best regards.

Yours faithfully,
Pyare Lal

(Reply to the Above)

Dear Pyare Lalji,

I am thrilled to receive your best wishes. To have Abhinav in my class was one of the most remarkable moments in my teaching career. It is true, as a teacher, we pay attention in equal measure to all the students, A few of them intelligently imbibe our dedication to teaching and achieve success, while other subdued ones fail to move along despite repetitive lectures.

Abhinav has truly made us proud in all respects. The crown of success rightly goes to Abhinav; besides the parents whose upbringing made him a star beyond compare!

Yours sincerely,
Nand Lal
Principal, Hindi Vidyalaya

(Sample-2)

Name and address of the sender
Dated…

Dear Vidyaji,

Pranam!

    I am at a loss of words to express my gratitude to you. Every single strand of my body is obliged to you. You have given me a new lease of life. Not only I, but the whole family is grateful to your benevolence. I will constantly look to be of some use to you, if ever the need arises.

Yours faithfully,
Nardev Dev

(Reply to the Above)

Name and address of the sender
Dated…

Dear Nardevji,

Pranam!

    Thank you for your kind letter. I am pleased to know that you are absolutely hale and hearty. In fact, your problem was old and chronic. That the medicines have helped you to get over the painful disease has given us confidence in the efficacy of our system of treatment.

    In fact, there is no reason for you to be grateful to us. It"s our basic duty. All I have done is to perform my duty.

Yours faithfully,
Ram Mani Vaidya

(Sample-3)

Name and address of the sender
Dated…

Dear Didi,

Pranam!

The kind of financial help extended to me is something I would never forget. I am truly obliged to you and Jijaji. It"s only due to your effort that my family could be resurrected. The business is progressing smoothly. I hope in the foreseeable future, I will be in a position to return the loan without any difficulty.

Rest all is fine.

Yours younger brother,
Sandeep

(Reply to the Above)

Name and address of the sender
Dated…

Dear Sandeep,

Love!

The kind of letter you have written has hurt us. Your Jijaji is equally sad. You were very young when you came under our care following the death of our mother. Both of us treated you like a child. I fail to understand how you summoned the courage to write such a letter.

Please don"t repeat this in future.

Yours sister,
Rajni

(Sample-1)

Obligatory Letters

Name and address of the sender

Dated…

The Director,

Education Department

Uttar Pradesh

Dear Sir,

Humbly I wish to state that by appointing me to the vacant post lying under your control, you have done a yeoman"s service to our whole family.

For this, I will ever remain grateful to you.

Yours faithfully,

Surya Pratap Singh

(Sample-2)

Name and address of the sender

Dated…

Dear Sir,

All the members of my family are grateful to you for saving our lives from fire. It was sheer providence that you were around. Otherwise, the restricted road space of the locality would have prevented fire tenders from reaching the area under fire. We are short of words to thank you.

We would be pleased to be of some service to you.

Yours faithfully,

Jeevan Prakash

(Sample-3)

Name and address of the sender
Dated...

Dear Sir,

   I am at a loss for words to express my gratitude to you for saving the life of my lone child unscathed out of the brutal fire that had engulfed the area. You have done what I couldn"t do as a father. People like you are rare who are prepared to sacrifice their comfort for the sake of others.

   I would be much obliged if I could be of some use to you now or ever.

Yours sincerely,
Navin

(Sample-4)

Social Obligatory Letter

Name and address of the sender
Dated...

Dear Sri Kumar Gandharvaji,

   Your classical music floored the residents of Delhi. It"s something people will recite for long. India truly feels proud of your achievement. You have taken the Indian Art to a height never achieved before.

   On behalf of all of Delhi, I extend our warmest thanks to you. I hope we all will relish and cherish the melodious recital for long.

On behalf of the citizens of Delhi,
Madan Mohan Mehta

(Sample-5)

Name and address of the sender
Dated…

Dear Madan Mohanji,

I am grateful for your kind letter. The recital which you, on behalf of the Delhi residents have appreciated and respectfully spoken is, in fact, one of the art form of India since ancient times. I am simply a practitioner of this art.

I feel personally obliged to you all for showering such a high regard. It would be remarkably wonderful if I get another opportunity to recite before the knowledgeable and appreciative people that the citizens of Delhi are known for.

Your sincerely,
Kumar Gandharva

(Sample-6)

Name and address of the sender
Dated…

Dear Acharyaji,

You have done a great service to the Hindi literature by wrting a history of Hindi Literature. No doubt, the history of Hindi literature written by Acharya Ramchandra Shukla is immortal but we have to appreciate that the subject of history is moving at a rapid pace. Today"s news becomes stale tomorrow. Hence, there is a growing need to rewrite and reflect the current history in the right perspective. You have done a brilliant job. On behalf of the lovers of Hindi, I am sending you a congratulatory letter.

I hope you would graciously accept our regards,

Yours sincerely,
Dinanath Bhargava

Name and address of the sender
Dated…

Dear Bhargavaji,

I am in receipt of your kind letter. The manner in which you have accepted my manuscript is a matter of great rejoice for me. I see no reason why you should be so grateful. As a matter of fact, I am just doing what I am expected to do as a writer. I am just serving the cause of Hindi literature.

Yours sincerely,
Dhirendra Prasad

(Sample-8)
(Reply)

Name and address of the sender
Dated…

Dear Sir,

Yesterday, I saw the working of your newly manufactured knitting machine at a factory. A designer cloth piece was being weaved on it. This kind of machine is going to help India manufacture some outstanding materials. I offer my sincere gratitude to you on behalf of the citizens of Palampur.

Yours sincerely,
Beni Madhav

Name and address of the sender
Dated...

Dear Beni Madhavji,

I am grateful for the appreciation you have shown. This machine has been designed basically for the propagation and working in rural areas. We hope weavers in rural areas would be benefitted immensely by working on it.

Yours sincerely,
D. Divakar

(Sample-10)

Name and address of the sender
Dated...

Dear Kamalji,

I hope you all are hale and hearty. The kind of service you have showered on people of this area during your three years of stay is simply outstanding. I am sure you will continue to extend your best wherever you go and live. I hope you will continue to guide us with your valuable suggestion at all times.

Yours sincerely,
Srinivas
Convenor,
District Congress Committee

(Reply)

Name and address of the sender

Dated…

Dear Srinivasji,

    I am thankful to you for your kind letter. During my three years of living with good people like you has strengthened our relationship to such an extent that I wouldn"t be able to forget it even if I wish to. The love extended by people of your area is beyond expression in words.

    I hope you and I will continue to have a cordial relationship as we had althrough.

Yours faithfully,

Kamal

Address

Date...

Letters of Obligation, Condolence, etc.

(Sample-1)
A Thank You Letter for Donating Books for the Library

Name and address of the sender
Dated:

Dear Dr. Kailashji,

We are grateful to you for donating our library a few rare books on Hindi literature. These books are generally not available in the market.

We are sure many readers who are desirous of reading these books would be greatly benefitted.

We value your contribution from the bottom of our hearts.

Regards,

Yours sincerely,
Anant 'Agaman"

(Sample-2)
Thanking a Person for Returning the Lost Papers

Name and address of the sender
Dated:

Dear Sri Mishraji,

When I placed an advertisement in the newspaper under the 'lost" column, I had hardly expected to get the papers back. Right now, when I got them back under an envelope, I was delightfully surprised. Although, we have never met, I get the feeling as if my elder brother is returning the same to me, while cautioning me to be more careful in future. We are totally at a loss when we discovered its loss during our bus journey. The papers included some important documents of my father besides other certificates. By promptly returning them, you have really won our hearts.

I have no words to express my gratitude. I am highly obliged to you and would certainly like to meet you whenever you have time. I look forward to meeting you soon.

Yours sincerely,
Chetan Singh

(Sample-3)
Condolence Letter to a Friend on the Death of his Mother

Name and address of the sender
Dated:

Dear Anil,

We all were stunned to hear the sudden demise of your mother. We had expected her to enjoy life for many more years. But then, who has control over destiny? Anyone who has come is destined to go one day. May God give you the strength to bear this irreparable loss! The whole village folks would feel the void caused by her absence. We can replace everything but our parents! Please take care to fulfil the wishes of your mother. Only that would be the best form towards your attempts to repay her debt, if that could be said.

May God let her soul rest in peace!

Your friend,
Karan Sood

(Sample-4)
Condolence Letter to a Friend on the Death of his Father

Name and address of the sender
Dated:

Dear Satishji,

We all were shocked to hear the sad news of the sudden demise of your father. It was hard to believe it happened so unexpectedly. We are at a loss for words to express our sense of pain. We are all insignificant in front of the Almighty. In such a situation, there is little anyone could do. Now, the entire responsibility has fallen on your shoulders. I hope you will be able to squarely meet them.

We were a close-knit member of the family. His sublime guidance was always available to us.

I pray to God to let his soul rest in peace and give you the strength to bear this irreparable loss.

Your friend,
Aman Kumar

(Sample-5)
Condolence Letter to a Friend on the Death of his Father

Name and address of the sender
Dated:

Dear Ajay,

My heart sank to hear the news of the sudden demise of your father this afternoon. It was really hard to believe it happened so unexpectedly. Just the last week when I was with you all, he conversed with me in an intimate tone and voice as if I was a close-knit member of the family. Truly, he was an epitome of love! His sublime nature and effervescence is hard to replicate.

It is true, time and tide wait for none. Death is beyond our control. It is destiny; one who has come is bound to go some day. Only difference is that some depart early while others wait a little longer.

Kindly gather the courage to bestow strength to your mother and little sister to bear this great loss. May God give each one of you strength to overcome the hard times; and peace to the departed soul!

I hope to reach your house soon.

Your friend,
Bhuvan

(Sample-6)
A Condolence Message

With a heavy heart, we inform you the untimely demise of our father, Dayanand Sharma on...

To perform the necessary rites for the departed soul, a meeting has been arranged at our house on Monday, dated........ from 9 – 11 in the morning and 4 – 6 in the evening.

Address
Residence

Surya Sharma
Aditya Sharma
Abhinav Sharma, and
the Sharma Family

Descriptive Letters

Now let us have a look at some of the personal letters. In this section, we will pay attention to only those letters which a person writes to his relatives or friends. These letters enquire about personal and family welfare. They don"t talk about commercial matters. The subject matter of these letters come from the heart and are broadly of four kinds. These are Descriptive, Emotional, Travel-related and General.

(Sample-1)
Descriptive Letters

Dear Rajni,

I trust mummy, papa and all the youngsters in the family are hale and hearty.

Ever since the time I read the glory of Taj Mahal, it has been my earnest desire to have a close look at this monument. I did decide to go to Agra many times, but the plan kept getting dropped for one reason or the other. Finally, I got an opportunity to visit Agra along with my school friends.

Taj Mahal occupies a unique place among the great monuments of the world. It represents symbolically the emotional integration of love and affection best reflected in the moonlit night. Many lovebirds profess their love for one another here in the surroundings of the beautiful Taj for all times to come.

The foreigners who visit India always try to fit-in and ensure to pay a visit to this great marvel of the Mughal architecture. This mausoleum built by Shah Jahan in memory of his beloved wife Mumtaz Mahal took more than 20 years to be built at an enormous cost of crores of rupees. This was built during the time of the great famine and its construction enabled many distressed hands to earn a living. The materials used were expensive white marbles and precious gems and stones cut to proper sizes.

Agra is situated on the bank of the River Yamuna. It flows from its rear side. The moment I entered the huge gate of the Taj Mahal, I was standing right in front of the the epoch-making monument of love that Shah Jahan had built. There were rows of trees lined up right from the gate till the monument"s entrance. Fountains enhanced the beauty.

We reached the monument and were literally blinded with its breath-taking white marbled setting. Tall minarets were erected at the four corners of the white marble-made square platform. A few went atop the minaret and had a panoramic view. The architecture simply left us wonderstruck.

Dear Rajni, what do I tell you about the art and craft on the monument and the minarets? I am absolutely at a loss for words. Eye-soothing paintings made it difficult to differentiate between the original and the fake ones. In the centre of the mausoleum, two graves have been built in memory of the great Mughal emperor Shah Jahan and his beloved Mumtaz. It is the place where lies, in eternity, the souls of the two great lovers.

Today happened to be the full moon day. I realise that the beauty of the Taj Mahal will stand in full glory for years to come. A few foreigners were also there who were nonplussed with its beauty as much as we were.

I wish you were also with me along with mummy. We all would have enjoyed the phenomenal beauty all the more. I hope to bring you along to visit Taj Mahal during this summer vacation.

Your loving brother,
Sagar

Agra

Dated:

(Sample-2)

Letter to a Younger Brother Suggesting Ways to Stay Healthy

Address:
Date:...............

Dear Sushil

Trust this finds you in cheers. I have received a letter from our mother. She is worried about your health. I know mothers are quite sentimental and worry about even small things. But there are some facts that do cause genuine worry. So I thought I should speak to you on this matter. Pay attention and you will not cause worry to anyone. Good nutrition is very important for health. Stay away from outside foods. These could be contaminated. While eating, try to remain cool and calm as tension leads to stress and this leads to many illnesses. And then sleep is equally important for seven hours every night. Staying awake till late hours causes irritation and ill-health. Getting up early is very healthy. And the third suggestion is exercise and physical activity. So many people go for Yoga. You must try to learn these from someone who knows it or try other forms of physical exercises that will always keep you fit. Jogging is very good to stay fit and fine in body and mind. A good physical health is reflected in equally good mental health. You must stay away from filthy literature and people who tend to spoil the mental make-up of a person. Just remember, if character is lost, everything is lost! Indulge in creative activities. A good health is for life. This is a capital which will stand by you for all times. Do let me know how you are keeping up with your health.

Your elder brother
Anurag

(Sample-3)

Writing a Letter to Chacha/Chachi Wanting to Spend Holidays with Them

Address:

Date:.......

Dear Chacha and Chachiji,

I trust you all are well. I wrote to you earlier that this Dussehra vacation, I want to spend with you. It has been quite some time I ate Panjiri made by Chachi. It would be kind of killing two birds with one stone. Sight-seeing and good food together. I may reach there by 14th of October. I have learnt that Bhubaneswar is a new city built over the old one. Besides spending two days is Bhubaneswar, I would like to visit Nandan Kanan also to see the tigers. A visit to the Buddha and the Jain caves and the Kalinga war remnants are also on the cards. Then we will visit to the magnificent Konark to see the Sun Temple. I would next proceed to Jagannath Puri to see the Jagannath Temple. Finally, I would also like to see the Dham, one of the four established by Shankaracharya. I look forward to spend a day on the Puri beach too. I have expressed my wish list, but I don"t know how many will actually fructify. Kindly fix a suitable time-slot as per your convenience. Convey my love to Alisha.

Your loving nephew,

Anubhav

(Sample-1)

Emotional Letters

Letter from a Pre-marriage Lover to his Beloved

Dear Deep

My life, my imagination beyond my dreams, Deep – I have become a kind of slave to you. In any direction, I look, I notice is you. Here there and everywhere. It appears you are mocking at my perplexity or wonderment. I just can"t describe the sense of fulfilment I get from these imaginary visuals. Here things have turned out a little worrisome as my so called sister, Astha has spread rumours (in fact, they are true) about our love for each other. My friend circle are pulling my leg. Every time, they drag me despite showing displeasure, I feel ecstatic. I am anxiously awaiting your mail. Take care!

Yours only

Anand

Delhi

Dated:........

(Reply)

Dear Anand

I received your letter. In fact, it was a poem in the shape of prose. I must be congratulated for transforming you into a poet. To tell you the truth, I have derived no pleasure by coming to Shimla from Delhi. Three days of wondering here without your company has sapped almost all the energy out of me. No enjoyment, no pleasure. Truly speaking, I have stopped going out. Shimla appears dry without you. Neither the mornings are pleasant nor are the evenings romantic. There is no youthful flurry either in the vegetations or in the mountains. The element of attraction is just not there in Shimla. Do you know why? It is just because of you are not here.

Yours always,
Deepshikha

Shimla

Dated:.......

(Sample-1)

Travel-Related Letter

My Haridwar Trip

Dear Sanjay,

India is a land of pilgrim centres. Slopes of mountains, rivers banks, ponds or sea-shores, you would find them everywhere. No wonder, foreigners describe India as a land of pilgrim centres. And Haridwar is one such popular centre.

Haridwar is situated on the banks of the River Ganges in the state of Uttarakhand. The Ganges flows down making way from the icy mountains of the Himalayas. The water is pure and icy cold. It is said that taking a dip in the river washes away the sins committed by us in the past. Though scientists discount this theory, nevertheless, they admit to acquiring enormous mental peace and tranquillity following a bath in the Ganges.

Despite Hardwar being is a small town, people from all parts of the country flock to this place. It is reckoned as a prominent city since times immemorial. A *mela* (fair) known as the 'Kumbh Mela" is organised every 12 years during which lakhs of people from every corner of the country visit to take a dip in the Holy River.

A number of temples are situated on the banks of the Ganges. There is a place called 'Har Ki Paudi", which is very popular among the pilgrims. This place was originally built on the bank of the Ganges, but now the river has changed its course and flows a little distance away from the site. However, a canal has been constructed at the 'Har Ki

Paudi" through which the river water still flows. A number of people gather at this spot every day. Temples of prehistoric times built to pay obeisance to Gangaji and Shivaji are worshipped since early morning till evening. After the sunset, people offer their prayers to Ganga *maiyya* and let off lit earthen lamps in the River Ganges. The scene presents a breathtaking view of the whole area. Thousands of pilgrims and visitors flock the place; to such an extent that literally no place is left to accommodate any more.

In the nearby hills are situated the temples of Mansa Devi and Chandi Devi. A ropeway exists to reach the Mansa Devi. We decided to make use of the aerial ropeway to visit the temple. It was a trip to remember. Our trolley stopped about 100 metres from the temple due to electrical problem. The moment was truly fearful. People began to panic. It was hard to comfort them. A peek down below was enough to send shivers down the spine. A quiet thought flowing river, series of hillocks and dense forests – all were contributing to the deadly heart-stopping moments. However, I that had the trolley not stopped, I wouldn"t have paid attention to nature"s posture. I mentally made a note and surmised that walking to the temple delivers a different kind of phenomenon altogether.

I admit to have made a number of pilgrimages, but I think I would never forget this heart-throbbing and eye-dropping experience of Haridwar.

I wish to visit this place with you in the coming season.

Yours affectionately,
Atul Saxena

Mixed Type of Letters

Letter writing is not a compartmentalised activity where you stay within a certain boundary. It depends upon who you are writing to. While business letters stay within defined parameters, personal letters, especially to close ones, overlap. While writing, some writers flow along and tend to mix up descriptive subjects with emotional or philosophical ones.

(Sample-1)
Letter to Wife

Dear Deepti,

I hadn"t been able to write to you for quite some time. Just work pressure and nothing else. However, this evening, I was feeling very lonely and hence, decided to go to India Gate. It"s very lovely to look at and quite impressive. Properly mowed lawns present an attractive scene. Fountains placed along and birds flocking along add to the serene beauty.

I came to visit this place but I just didn"t enjoy one bit. I always thought of telling you as and when I passed any attractive place or scene. But well, there was none to speak to. I, perforce, had to keep my mouth shut.

I was simply bored of not having you by my side. I wish you were there with me. Despite my best efforts, I couldn"t enjoy the visit.

Next time, when you are here, I will make sure we go together and enjoy the beauty of the place.

Rest all is fine!

Yours,
Sagar

Delhi

Dated: ....

(Sample-2)

A Letter to Husband

My Dearest,

I trust you are hale and hearty. We reached Banaras yesterday from Allahabad. We went to the Sarnath temple. The temple is very attractive to look at, but the statue of Bhagwan Buddha was beyond description. The paintings and images inscribed on the walls attract one from a distance. These paintings describe the prominent legacy of the life of Bhagwan Buddha.

The place is truly praiseworthy. You just won"t tire roaming around. The still existing remnants at the place reflect the relic of the glory of the bygone days.

Dear, it was a visit hardly worth remembering simply because of your absence. I couldn"t enjoy the boat ride either, the kind we had last year during our Banaras trip. How mesmerising was that boat ride – a one in a lifetime affair! Can one ever forget that?

Yours lovingly,
Ananya Angrish

Banaras

Dated:

Letter from a Student to a Teacher

Dear Sir,

The time I left Allahabad, I had hoped to travel throughout the country. But in the middle of my trip, I reached such an important place where I needed to stay for some time. It is Delhi. The place is situated on the bank of River Yamuna. I wish to understand the culture, its people and the surroundings. I am writing below whatsoever information I have been able to gather about the city. I hope you will apprise me with your ideas.

Delhi today is a huge metropolis. For all practical purposes, Delhi now is a conglomeration of a number of towns and cities. It reflects the architecture and beauty of an old city superimposed by a new one. It is a city where you would find people of different cultures thoughtprocesses, different ethos and religions and from different towns and cities. Everyone seems to be free to choose any vocation or profession. No restriction is imposed on anyone. Despite the city boasting of everything, there is no emotional attachment, and hardly any intimacy, closeness and co-existence. It is a highly individualistic, concrete jungle, literally no one to share your views, opinions and thoughts. Just work and very little scope for personal life.

This realisation about materialism confounded me no end. The government says the city is truly on way to bigger things in life. It has progressed much and is close to final destination. But what one observes is that there is tremendous disaffection among people, discontentment is on the rise, intolerance is touching new heights and there is distrust all through.

Sir, there is nothing that can"t be achieved under your guidance. I need your guidance to dispel the misgivings about this great city crossing my mind. Kindly enlighten me with your thoughts how to go about interpreting the values that Delhi professes and represents.

Yours obediently,
Jai Prakash

Okhla, Delhi
Dated:

SELF-HELP/PERSONALITY DEVELOPMENT
(आत्म-सुधार/व्यक्तित्व विकास)

 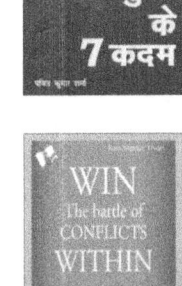   

SELF IMPROVEMENT
(आत्म विकास)

ENGLISH IMPROVEMENT
(अंग्रेजी सुधार)

STRESS MANAGEMENT (तनाव मुक्ति)

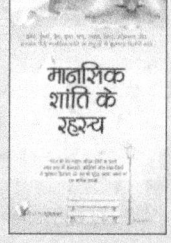

CAREER & BUSINESS MANAGEMENT
(कॅरियर एण्ड बिजनेस मैनेजमेंट)

JOB RELATED
(नौकरी सम्बन्धी)

Contact us at sales@vspublishers.com

STUDENT DEVELOPMENT/LEARNING
(छात्र विकास/लर्निंग)

MAGIC & FACT (जादू एवं तथ्य)

MUSIC (संगीत)

COMPUTER

Quiz Books
(प्रश्नोत्तरी की पुस्तकें)

MYSTERIES
(रहस्य)

DRAWING BOOKS (ड्राइंग बुक्स)

 **QUOTES/SAYINGS (उद्धरण/सूक्तियाँ)**

BIOGRAPHIES (आत्म कथाएँ)

 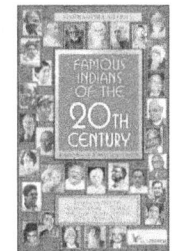

PUZZLES (पहेलियाँ)

     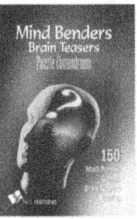

ACTIVITIES BOOK (एक्टिविटीज बुक)

Contact us at sales@vspublishers.com

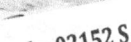